MEGA GIRAF

S0-ABC-643

MegaCityVille

MEGA HEN

MEGA WOLF

UNNY

MEGA MOUSE

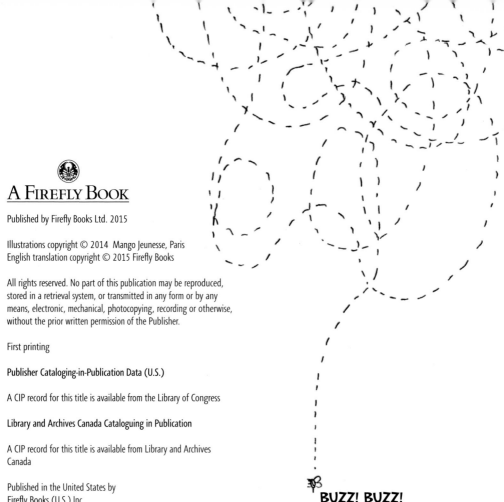

A FIREFLY BOOK

Published by Firefly Books Ltd. 2015

Illustrations copyright © 2014 Mango Jeunesse, Paris
English translation copyright © 2015 Firefly Books

First printing

Publisher Cataloging-in-Publication Data (U.S.)

A CIP record for this title is available from the Library of Congress

Library and Archives Canada Cataloguing in Publication

A CIP record for this title is available from Library and Archives
Canada

Published in the United States by
Firefly Books (U.S.) Inc.
P.O. Box 1338, Ellicott Station
Buffalo, New York 14205

Published in Canada by
Firefly Books Ltd.
50 Staples Avenue, Unit 1
Richmond Hill, Ontario L4B 0A7

Printed in China

BUZZ! BUZZ!

MEGA ☆ PIG

SÉVERINE VIDAL

BARROUX

How Mega Pig
crushed Mosquito Man

FIREFLY BOOKS

This is Mega Pig!
It's easy to recognize him:
he has a special corkscrew tail.

He is the pinkest of the Mega Animals!

He lives in a house that he shares with his two brothers.
He has the smallest room but...the biggest closet!

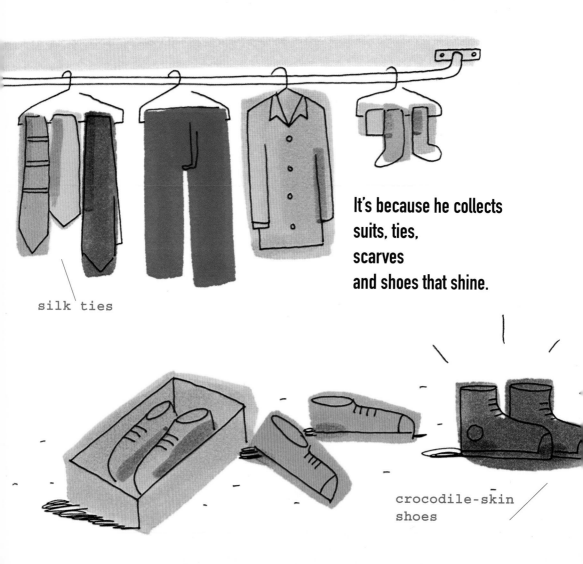

silk ties

It's because he collects
suits, ties,
scarves
and shoes that shine.

crocodile-skin
shoes

He's not like other pigs:
mud fights are not his thing.

Mega Pig is always very elegant.

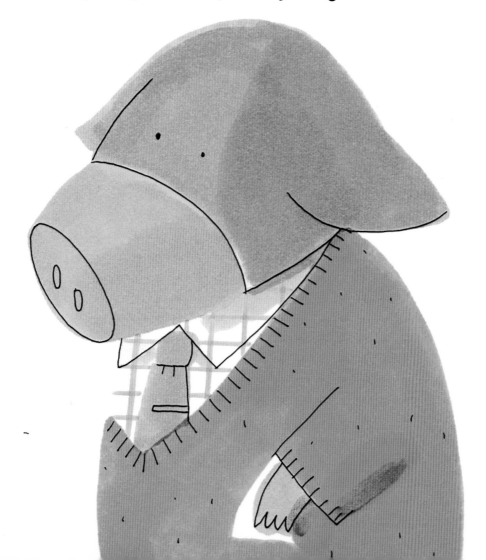

In short, let's say that Mega Pig
is very classy, spotless from head to hoof.
He changes outfits three times a day.
Everyone in town knows this.

Everyone also knows
 that he's a black belt in karate.

Thanks to his kimono and his Mega powers,
he KOs his enemies, even the dreadful
Mosquito Man, the Big Wicked Mosquito
thirsty for blood.

Today, it's a celebration in the streets of MegaCityVille.
Mega Pig dances the mambo with Mega Mouse.

But Mosquito Man buzzes looking to stir up trouble!

I hate celebrations,
I'm going to rain on this parade!

Mosquito Man can't stand it anymore,
he's in the mood for a great big fight.

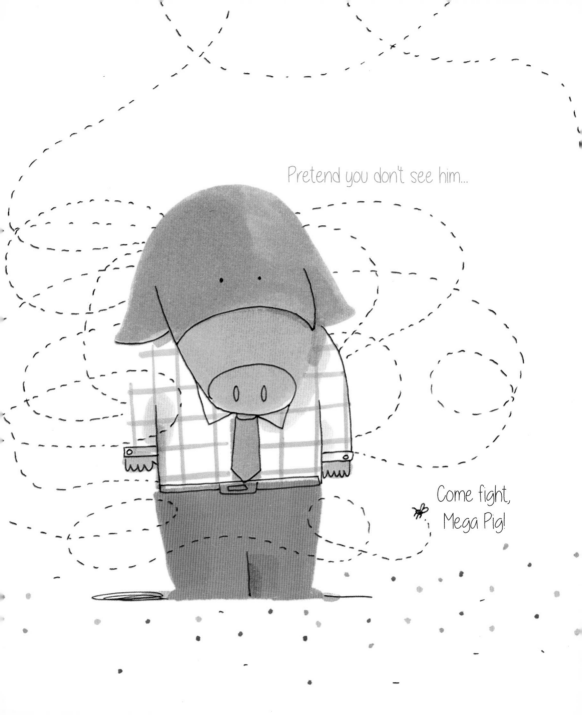

The evil Mosquito Man is determined:
He wants to bite Mega Mouse.
Right there, just behind her right ear.

Mega Pig tries to remain calm:
"Go play somewhere else Mosquito Man!"

Mosquito Man picks up the ketchup
and aims for Mega Pig!
"There! Take that!"
shouts Mosquito Man.

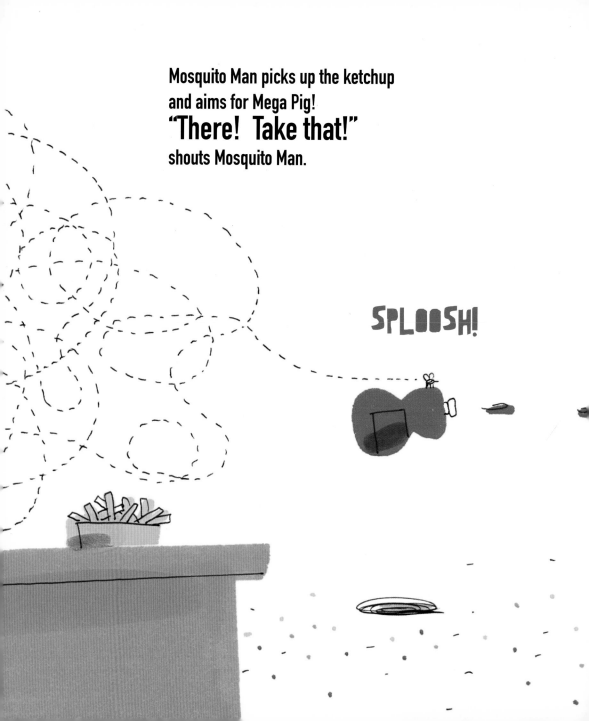

SPLOOSH!

Mega Pig is very upset.
He is horrified of stains, especially red ones.

Mega Pig is so upset that he jumps into action!

KO'd in three seconds flat by Mega Pig!

Thanks to Mega Pig, the party can continue.

I'll be back!

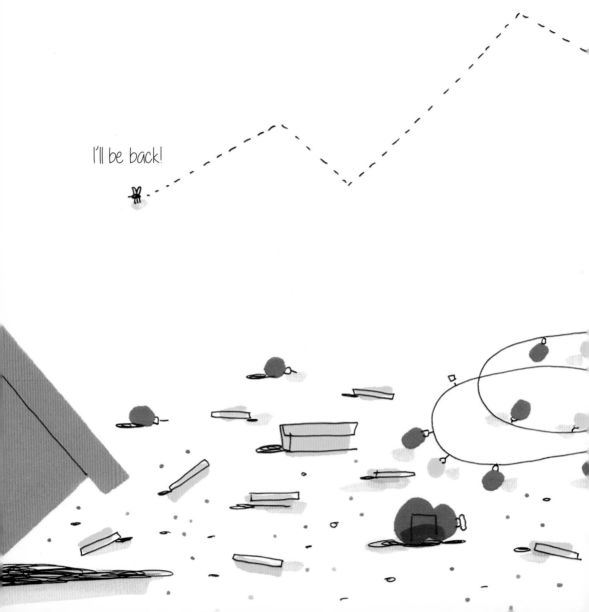

Well! That's it for me, I'm going home to do laundry!

Nothing works better against a ketchup stain than a good machine washing...

Oh no! My shirt shrank! It's ruined!

Poor Mega Pig! The day had started so well!

Mega Pig certainly wants to save the world from time to time, or crush Mosquito Man...

But his favorite thing of all is to eat jam
from a spoon in front of the TV...

Shhh...it's a secret

MEGA BEAR

MOSQUITO MAN

MEGA PIG

MEGA CROC

MEGA PANDA

MEGA HIPPO